TO
ELLA,
LOVE FROM

......................Nanny...x

On a normal street like yours and mine,
It was a bright and sunny day.
Ella opened the door, and suddenly saw,
A gang of animals waiting to play.

The tiger loves taking centre stage,
He's quite the confident one.
But equally, and I'm sure you'll agree,
His shy friends are also fun.

Hide-and-seek's a favourite game,
It's Ella versus the giraffes.
Her careful disguise won't fool their eyes,
And it ends with smiles and laughs.

Some friends like to relax and snuggle,
Others creep about and are tickly.
The otters hug, the gorillas are snug,
And the porcupines are cute and prickly.

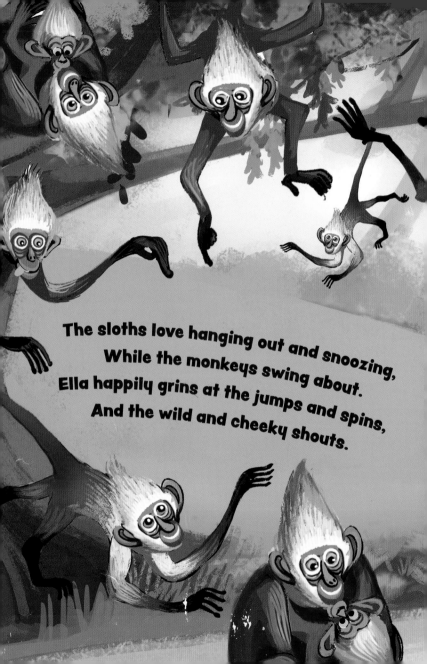

The sloths love hanging out and snoozing,
While the monkeys swing about.
Ella happily grins at the jumps and spins,
And the wild and cheeky shouts.

It's time to settle down for lunch,
Ella's burger takes some beating.
Her friends have FRUITS,

GRASS, GRUBS and ROOTS,

GROSS! What's the dung beetle eating?!

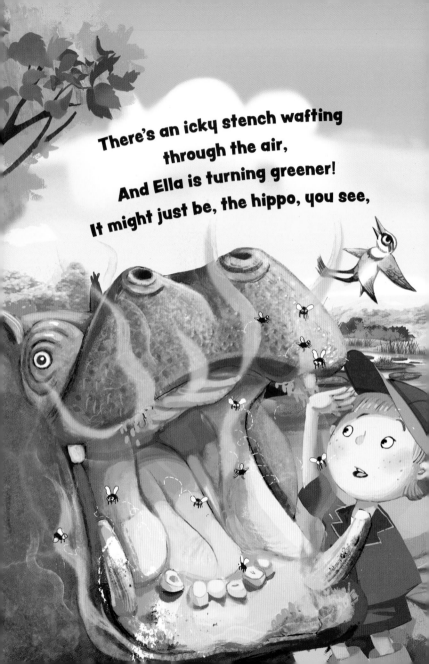

There's an icky stench wafting
through the air,
And Ella is turning greener!
It might just be, the hippo, you see,

Ella spots the rhinos squabbling,
They're bickering and butting their heads.
She must put a stop, to their childish strop,
"I'll try a spot of juggling," she said.

Ella's hair is a little bit messy,
"But my friends look much funnier!"
she thinks.

They're **BUSHY** and **BRISTLY**, **SPIKY** and **FRIZZY**,
All coloured red, orange and pinks.

The giraffe takes flight,
And the hippo's a sight,
As they LEAP and
BOUNCE and SPRING.

Night night,
ELLA

Ella is ready to head back home,
As night eclipses the day.
But there's still time,
For a little more rhyme,
As her friends have

SOMETHING TO
SAY....

Ella, now draw your different friends and tell us why they're so special.

Written by Joe Barnes
Illustrated by Cinzia Battistel
Designed by Alice Xavier

First published by HOMETOWN WORLD in 2019
Hometown World Ltd
1 Queen Street
Bath
BA1 1HE

Visit

www.hometownworld.co.uk

Follow us @hometownworldbooks

 Hometown World